NO LOVE FOR SCHNITZEL

Bets Benedict did not like dogs. In a house that boasted four Irish setters and one dachshund, she had the only room that was strictly off limits for all four-footed beasts. It was clean and neat and she intended to keep it that way. Then one day her grandmother arrived with a special surprise: she had signed a lease for an apartment in New York City without noticing the no dog clause and now she must find a home for her aging dachshund, Schnitzel. Eleven-year-old Bets had been elected the new owner. This is the story of how "No Love for Schnitzel" turns into lots of love for Schnitzel. After many adventures—at a pet show, in South Carolina hunting doves, and just playing together—Bets and Schnitzel become inseparable. The climax comes when the brave little dog saves Bets and her sister, Corky, from real disaster—and nearly loses her own life in the effort.

No Love for Schnitzel

By **Suzanne Wilding**

Illustrated by **Sam Savitt**

St Martin's Press   NEW YORK

Also by Suzanne Wilding:
DREAM PONY FOR ROBIN

Text copyright © Suzanne Wilding Berol, 1963
Illustrations copyright © St Martin's Press, Inc., 1963
All rights reserved
Library of Congress Catalog Card Number: 63-9424
MANUFACTURED IN THE UNITED STATES OF AMERICA

TO MYRA,
whose help and understanding
know no bounds

NO LOVE FOR SCHNITZEL

Chapter 1

"Hey Bets, Granny's here!" Corky, my older sister bounced into the room followed by Bitsy, her ugly dachshund.

"She's got a great surprise for you!" Corky gave me a funny look and parked herself on my bed. Bitsy jumped up beside her.

Outside, the Irish setters were barking. Thank the Lord, Corky had left them behind.

"Get that sausage off my bed! Mine's the only

clean room in the house and I intend to keep it that way."

"If that's the way you want it." Corky picked herself up, whistled to Bitsy and stalked out of the room.

"What's the surprise?" I called after her, but a banging door was my answer.

What can Granny be bringing me? It isn't my birthday and she is much too busy selling her house in Scarsdale and moving to New York to go on a shopping spree.

I ran a comb through my short hair, tightened the belt of my slacks, and pulled my sweater down. I'd look neat at least. That's more than you could say for Corky. She is a slob and proud of it: plump, messy, and always late. When I'm as old as Corky, I'll look like a lady and smell like one. Corky usually looks like a tramp and smells like a kennel. What would happen to my pretty room if Bitsy had the run of it? All she does is sit on the furniture and scratch. Bet she's full of fleas.

I closed my room door carefully and hurried

downstairs. I love our house; it's old, comfortable, shabby, and lived in by four people and five dogs. Mom, Pop, and Corky adore the beasts. I'm the only one who doesn't. I don't exactly hate them, but they're such pests; always messing up the house, dashing down the stairs, scattering the rugs, and barking at the slightest sound.

I straightened the hall runner and turned into the parlor, a pleasant panelled room, loaded with comfortable furniture covered in green chintz.

Mom and Granny were talking earnestly. "Hope Betsy won't disappoint us," I heard Granny say.

"But I feel sorry for . . ." My entrance interrupted her sentence.

"Hi Granny, what brings you here?" I kissed her and snuggled close. She looked so worried.

"I thought you were busy packing?"

"I am." Granny moved uncomfortably in the armchair which looked small when she sat on it. She was a heavy woman but pretty and well dressed.

NO LOVE FOR SCHNITZEL

"The packers are coming this afternoon, but I'm here on an errand." She looked to Mom for support.

Schnitzel, Granny's old dachshund, as if sensing my grandmother's unhappiness, heaved herself into her mistress' lap.

"I brought you something special," Granny said pointing to a little box on the desk, but the package was so small that all I could see were Corky's and my pictures. They were taken for Dad's birthday and I didn't think much of them. Corky's wasn't bad, but I looked like a scrawny, green-eyed kid, blinking at the camera.

I started to open the gift . . .

"Granny has come to ask you a favor, Bets."

"Me, a favor?" I couldn't imagine what.

"Do you want me to help you move?" I didn't know what good an eleven-year-old would be, but I was sure that since Grandpa's death several months ago, Granny was often lonely.

"No Betsy, it's a much bigger favor than that." Granny absentmindedly stroked Schnitzel. "You're always supposed to read the fine print in any document, but I must have left my glasses home. I didn't notice the no dog clause when I signed the lease for my new apartment. There was a quiver in Granny's voice. "I can't take Schnitzel and I have to find a good home for her."

I nodded sympathetically. But why talk with me about it?

"I want you to take her." There were tears in Granny's eyes as she spoke.

"Me!" I was horrified.

"Corky has her own dog and your mother is surrounded by Irish setters. If she's yours, I know you'll look after her. She's used to a lot of love, but she isn't spoiled. She's never been allowed on the furniture, only on my lap." Granny smiled.

I couldn't help but think of the talk I had had with Mom that very morning. "A room is meant to be lived in," Mom had said. "If we have dogs in the house, we'll stick to washable, dark fabrics."

"But light colors are much prettier!"

"Don't complain, Bets," she had answered

laughingly. "Your room is the way you want it: pale yellow and gray. It's the only non dog proof room in the house."

"But Granny, I'm no good with dogs." The last thing in the world I wanted was to get stuck with Schnitzel. "And I'm at school all day!"

"Give it a try, Bets. Granny's done lots of favors for you. In time, you may enjoy having a dog as a companion." Mom gave me no choice. She picked the old dog off Granny's lap and put her on the floor next to me. "You'll do alright," she said, giving me a quick hug. "Just give Schnitzel half a chance."

The little, old dog looked questioningly at me and then at Granny, but Granny looked the other way.

I patted her gingerly, called her by name, and wondered if she would follow me?

Not a chance! She jumped back onto Granny's lap and sat there shaking. I didn't want her, and she wanted no part of me.

Now Mom took over. "Where's the leash?"

she inquired. Granny fumbled around in the chair. Mom clipped it on Schnitzel's collar and handed it to me. "Now Betsy, take her to your room." There was no nonsense in her voice.

I tried, but Schnitzel sat down and wouldn't budge. "I can't just drag her!" I was almost in tears now.

Mom picked up the dog and put her in my arms. "I guess you'd better carry her," she said quietly.

Chapter 2

Schnitzel's whining awakened me at six the following morning. "She's at it again," I mumbled to myself, but it couldn't be as bad as yesterday afternoon. She had howled, sulked, not touched her food and had looked so miserable that I was willing to try anything to cheer her up, but she would have none of me.

I opened half an eye and saw the metal bed that Granny had left for her, empty; her blanket strewn across the floor like a discarded parachute, and Schnitzel, her nose glued to the door, scratching to get out.

"Granny's gone," I said not too unkindly. "Stop making so much fuss. I want to sleep . . . it's Saturday." No use! The moment she realized that I was awake, she ran to my bed and then to the door. In desperation she tore at the woodwork with her squat, brown paws, now flecked with gray.

I stuck my head under the blanket and tried to sleep, but she was insistent. "Have it your own way," I mumbled grudgingly. I pulled my warm dressing gown over my pajamas, felt around for my slippers and opened the door. She was down the stairs as fast as her stocky legs would carry her, past the front door and to the parlor.

She stopped short in front of the chair where Granny had sat. She wrinkled her brow, and sniffed and sniffed with her nearly white muzzle.

Slowly, she circled the room, her tail dragging, her long ears hanging limply. She cased the parlor, the hall, the dining room, and the kitchen. But Granny was nowhere to be found.

She was an awful nuisance, but I couldn't help feeling sorry for her. I opened the front door and out she went . . . but not for long. She came back, walked resolutely upstairs, made a straight line for her blanket, which had been Granny's old scarf, and carried it to her bed.

I breathed a sigh of relief and crawled back under the covers, shortly to be awakened again. This time the racket came from under my bed. I hung over the edge and looked beneath. There was my new charge scratching up my beautiful, thick, birthday-present rug.

"Stop that!" I commanded. "What do you think you're doing. Digging for oil?"

Schnitzel looked up, surprised at being spoken to so sharply, and gave me a hurt look. She gathered up Granny's scarf, which I guess she was trying to bury, and slunk back to her basket.

I started to dress. No point doing anything else. What was I going to do with the pest? In one night, she'd scratched up my door, tried to tear up my carpet, and ruined my Saturday morning snooze. I straightened the room and finally opened my present. It had been forgotten in yesterday's excitement. Granny always brought us gifts, but this one was extra special: a gold dachshund for my charm bracelet. I snapped the box shut, stuck it in my bureau, and glared at Schnitzel. She avoided my gaze and looked into space. "The feeling is mutual," I said.

Glancing into the mirror, I brushed my short brown hair. "Betsy Benedict, you monster," I scolded myself. "Everybody likes dogs except you." I shook my head. What was I to do about it?

I could hear Corky talking to Bitsy in her room. The shower was running full tilt in Mom and Pop's bathroom and the big dogs were charging down the stairs for their morning outing. As long as I was up, I might as well go down and start breakfast for Mom.

"What a nice surprise," she kissed the top of my head. "I have an assistant this morning." Mom was dressed for a Saturday on the farm with Dad. Her frontier pants looked tight, but trim, and her fluffy wool sweater was warm and cosy. She looked good in anything. She combed her hair, pageboy style. It's the easiest and the neatest," she'd often explain.

"How was your room-mate?" she inquired.

My face must have told her, for she quickly said, "You've got to be patient. Schnitzel is an old dog; it will be hard for her to get used to your ways."

"Do I have to keep her, Mom?"

"You have to give it a try. Stop worrying and bring me the pancake batter. Your father likes a good breakfast on week-ends."

I could hear Dad letting the dogs out. They weren't allowed in the kitchen.

"Morning, Bets," Dad called as he headed for the breakfast nook. "How's our new dog trainer?" He drank his juice and picked up the paper. Perhaps he wouldn't notice if I didn't answer that difficult question.

NO LOVE FOR SCHNITZEL

I brought the first batch of pancakes to the table and gave them to Dad. He loved to eat and made Corky mad, 'cause he never had to watch his weight.

Whenever she complained, he always said, "If you worked in the garden and with the chickens and steers, you might be able to eat more without worrying." The farm is Dad's hobby, but selling cars in New York City is his business. Today, he looked like a real farmer in jeans, work shoes and a plaid shirt. But real farmers don't read the *New York Times,* and my Dad's day is spoiled if he doesn't find it on the breakfast table.

Dad folded the paper and looked at me thoughtfully. "You don't mind that little dog, do you?" he inquired.

"She's a pest and she's ruining my room!"

He glanced at me sharply. "Getting an old dog used to new surroundings is hard work, and you've never liked dogs, especially big ones." He poured more syrup on his pancakes. "The setters used to push you down the stairs when you were little and scared you. I think you're still afraid of them."

I fiddled with my pancakes. "Well sometimes," I admitted grudgingly, "but . . ."

Dad wandered out to the kitchen.

"This dog routine is going to be rough on Betsy," I heard him tell Mom.

"But she'll come around," Mom answered confidently. "She's kind hearted, and living with Schnitzel may make her get over her fear of big dogs."

So that's what was in back of it all. I'd like not to be afraid, but Schnitzel wouldn't change that. Wish Granny had given me a dachshund charm and left it at that.

"Bets, come and see what your dog is doing!" Corky shouted excitedly from upstairs.

Bitsy and the big dogs had started to bark and now the din was unearthly.

I rushed upstairs two steps at a time and found Schnitzel guarding my room. Bitsy had wanted to snoop, but Schnitzel wouldn't let her over the door sill.

Attracted by the yipping, the Irish setters backed their friend. Five against one, but Schnitzel barred the way. She snarled her defiance and held her ground.

"Have you ever seen a braver dog?" Corky called out to me.

Skirting the pack, I managed to get in and close the door on our enemies.

"You're a good girl, at least you don't let other dogs mess up our room."

Schnitzel looked at me in surprise and wagged her tail slightly.

"Do you really mean it?" she seemed to say.

I patted her. After all, it wasn't her fault that Granny had dumped her on me. "We might as well be friends," I said. "It'll be a lot easier for both of us."

Having a dog of my own, mightn't be too bad, if Schnitzel would keep the monsters away. Whistling happily, I tidied up her bed, put fresh water in her bowl, and decided to take her for a walk.

The phone rang. I dashed into Mom's room.

It was Granny. "How'd my old girl make out last night?" was her first question.

Schnitzel had followed me and recognized Granny's voice. She sat up and tried to beg, but couldn't quite make it. She just managed to rock back and forth.

"Talk to her, Granny."

I held the receiver to her ear and the little dog cried with pleasure.

"Be a good girl," Granny finally said, "and I'll come and visit you soon."

I hung up, but Schnitzel didn't understand. She sat and stared at the instrument, hoping to hear more of Granny's voice.

"Come on Schnitzel," I pleaded. Granny will call soon again." But Schnitzel wouldn't move.

"Come on girl. Please come with me."

I put my arms around her and tried to comfort her. She licked my hand absentmindedly. What was I going to do with her?

Chapter 3

This time the scarf-blanket routine didn't work. Schnitzie was going to remain by the phone and that was that. I brought the tired old scarf in, showed it to her, and then slowly dragged it in front of her nose. I pretended I was a bull fighter; the old blanket, my cape, and Schnitzel, the bull. But my bull wouldn't follow the cape. She just looked at me sadly and whined.

I felt so sorry for Schnitzel that for two days

I brought her food and when necessary carried her outdoors.

Mom watched the goings on, but said nothing. "It'll be good for Betsy to work this one out," I heard her tell Dad.

My arms hurt from carrying my charge up and down stairs. She was small, but solid and weighed a ton. I was getting behind in my homework and hardly had time to tidy up and dust my room.

Corky isn't usually much help, but this time she came to the rescue. "Instead of taking Schnitzel out, let's give the dachshunds a real walk. Perhaps it'll get your mutt's mind off the telephone."

"She won't follow."

"Put her on a leash and once we get away from the house, I bet she'll stay with us."

I clipped the leather strap onto Schnitzel's collar and carried her downstairs.

"If you have to keep on lugging that dog, you'll get so scrawny that nothing will fit you."

"You're just jealous," I answered grumpily.

"You'll never have to worry about getting too thin."

Corky gave me a dirty look and opened the front door. Outside it was brisk and cold. She buttoned up her jacket, stuck her hands in her pockets and whistled to Bitzel.

Schnitzel walked sedately along side of me, but paid little attention to Bitzel frolicking in front of us. She acted dull and disinterested, but the sit-down-strike seemed to be over.

"Let's look at the mail box," Corky suggested. I hear someone has been fooling with it again."

"Okay, but then you'd better put Bitzel on a leash too. Mom says it's bad to take dogs down to the gate and give them the idea of going out on the road."

"Sure thing."

We walked toward Corky's mail box in silence. A sculptor friend of the family gave it to her for her birthday and the postmaster said it was okay to use. Ours is the only dachshund box in captivity; the head opens to hold letters and the tail stands up to notify the postman of out-going mail.

The box it cute, but the neighborhood kids are always trying to snitch it. Corky fiddled around with the brass dog, and then, satisfied that it was in good shape, walked down the road a few feet toward our back entrance.

Schnitzel pepped up a little. She sniffed at the myrtle covered bank, barked at a cat sunning himself on a neighbor's wall, and followed after Bitzel. As soon as we turned toward the vegetable garden, Corky unleashed Bitsy. Schnitzel looked up at me with her deep set eyes, "You can trust me," she seemed to say. "I won't run off." I unfastened the leash. She wiggled her tail slightly and trotted along.

We passed the red cattle shed filled with contented steers. The dachshunds sniffed around and then started to dig. The smell was delicious and the digging proceeded briskly.

"We'd better call them off, before they uproot the barn." Corky giggled at the prospect.

It was rather ridiculous to think of two little dogs wrecking a shed, but they sure knew how to dig. Bitsy, her nose down the hole, led the excavation. Schnitzie, her gray paws working feverishly, assisted.

We moved along and with a little persuasion, the dogs followed. We passed the workshop and the chicken house and walked toward the hay field. The dachsies were having fun scurrying through the autumn leaves, barking at a squirrel, giving tongue after an imaginary rabbit and trailing each other through the cow pasture.

It was great to be out. The dogs were interesting, the weather right, and the country beautiful. "May and October are the best months of the year. They make commuting worth-while," Dad always said, and we were in October.

Our apple trees, some still heavy with fruit, others picked clean, lined the back road. Frost hadn't spoiled the greeness of the fields and beyond them the woods were radiant with color, countless shades of reds, browns, and greens vied with each other for dominance. The dry fallen leaves crunched beneath our feet and rustled mysteriously as the dachshunds nosed through the underbrush.

They plunged into the thicket and hunted busily. We waited at the edge wondering whether Bitzel and Schnitzel would find any birds home.

"Schnitzel doesn't know anything about hunting. She never met a pheasant in Granny's Scarsdale garden."

"Wait and see. Instinct is what counts!" Corky sounded too wise for words.

She was right. In short order, a pair of pheasants squawked their annoyance and swooshed off into the woods.

"I told you dachshunds were all-purpose hunting dogs." Corky grinned delightedly and whistled to Bitzel.

"Let's go on," Corky volunteered. "The bridge in the woods isn't far."

I was tempted. "No," I finally said. "You know that Mom and Dad don't like us to go in the woods alone. The wild dogs haven't been seen lately, but I wouldn't want to meet up with them."

"I don't believe there are any!"

"Well I don't know. It would be different if

we had the setters with us. They could protect us."
Corky was undecided. Finally she turned toward
home. "Call your dog and let's head for the house."

Schnitzel came up to me, rubbed her nose on
my knee length socks, thumped her tail happily, and
scurried off after Bitzel.

"What an improvement! I bet you won't have
any more trouble with her now."

"She sure looks happier. Perhaps she'll settle
down and become part of the family."

We walked up the hill, climbed through the
post and rail fence, over the back lawn, and into
the house. The dachshunds stopped in the hall,
drank thirstily from the dog bowl, and then followed us upstairs. As she reached the top step,
Schnitzel stopped. Suddenly she remembered.

She looked first toward me and then toward
Mom's room and the telephone. Bitzel trailed after
Corky, only Schnitzel remained undecided.

Unconsciously I held my breath. Corky turned,
her eyes glued on Schnitzel. I crossed my fingers
and said a little prayer. Would she follow me?

Chapter 4

I stepped into my room, but Schnitzel did not move. I called to her. For a moment she hesitated, but then she came. I petted her and scratched her ears. She looked pleased.

From now on she slept in my room curled up in Granny's scarf and unlike Bitzel never once tried to take over the arm chair. Every morning before school I'd shake out her scarf-blanket, tidy up her bed, and give her fresh drinking-water. While I was gone, she'd wander around the house, stay with Bitzel or the big dogs, and bother no one.

34

I fed her after school, sometimes took her for a walk, and had plenty of time for my room and my homework. The daytime was easy, but sometimes the nights were bad. She'd lie in her bed, her head and paws resting on her blanket, and whine softly. That didn't wake me, but occasionally she'd let out a long mournful howl. Then I would put her bed next to mine, talk to her and hope that she would settle down.

"See that she's well exercised," was Mom's advice, "then she'll sleep better at night." But today I couldn't take her for her after school walk. Mom was giving a tea and Corky and I were her assistants.

The dogs had been banished from the house. The big dogs in the workshop and the dachshunds in the garage. For once it wouldn't hurt them to wait for their supper.

As the school bus dropped us at our gate, we dashed into the house and changed our clothes. Corky and I wore our new wool dresses. She looked trim and almost pretty. I loved my warm red dress and so did Mom. "Very becoming," she told me when I tried it on, "but why don't you grow a little. You can't wear size eight for ever."

"She's so sweet and petite," I'd heard Mrs. Jones tell Mom the other day. "Is she as fragile as she looks?"

"Don't kid yourself," my mother had answered laughingly. "Bets is as tough as steel and has a whim of iron."

What was I really like? I often wondered. I was strong and could keep up with Corky, but nothing ever bothered her and I was often unsure and sometimes afraid. My room was my castle and there I was queen. Schnitzel bothered me at first, but castles can be lonely and she was good company.

I gave my hair a final brushing and clipped on my charm bracelet. The gold dachshund jangled gaily. Somehow it made me feel good. "Stop primping," I told myself, "and get to work. You're needed downstairs."

Most of the guests had arrived and Corky was already passing cakes and sandwiches. Two of Mom's friends were pouring tea and coffee so that Mom was free to play hostess. I quickly pitched in. Emptying ash trays was my chore.

NO LOVE FOR SCHNITZEL

The house was dressed up with bowls of colored leaves and berries. Corky and I were good pickers and collecting greenery for the party made our dachshund walks more interesting.

"Let's open the porch door," Corky whispered to me. "Those dames sure heat up the joint."

"Good idea!" I snuck a brownie in my mouth and took a breather. The cigaret smoke was getting me down and a little fresh air would help. I'd visit the dachshunds, they were probably lonely. I headed for the garage, but it was empty. Mom couldn't have shut the door tightly and the two sausages had wiggled their way out. They were used to their afternoon walk—maybe they had decided to go on their own. They wouldn't go far without us. Most likely they were at the barn or the chicken house where the sounds and smells were always interesting.

Should I go and look for them, or should I return to the house? Better get back, I finally decided, Mom might need me. The dogs will have to take care of themselves.

The party was at its peak. Everyone was fed

and Corky and I had time to chat with Mom's friends. It wasn't much fun to talk with grown-ups, but Mom liked us to do it. The afternoon dragged on. It would be an hour at least before the guests started to leave.

"I don't know how your Mother does it," Aunt Jane was saying. "A house full of dogs and yet every thing is spotless and so pretty." She looked admiringly around the dining room.

"Mom says we have a dog-proof house." I'd hardly gotten the words out . . . when I heard Mom's horrified voice calling us. "Corky, Betsy come here immediately!"

We rushed into the parlor and there in the middle of the rug stood Bitzel and Schnitzel. I didn't need to look, my nose told me all. Cow manure! The smell was terrible. The dachsies were covered from head to tail and everytime they moved, large brown stains showed on the rug. They tried to be sociable, but the guests backed away from them.

"Get your dogs out of here pronto." Mom commanded.

We dragged the dachshunds out on the porch and slammed the door, but the damage was done.

"Quick into the garage with them." Corky took it calmly.

I held my nose with one hand and dragged Schnitzel with the other.

"We'll change our clothes and give them a bath. Otherwise the whole house'll stink!"

I dashed upstairs. My new dress was soiled and I smelled like a cow barn. I should have stuck to my guns. Dogs are terrible! Why did I ever get mixed up with one?

I kicked off my shoes, tossed my bracelet on the bureau, dumped my dress on the floor, and grabbed my jeans and turtle neck.

"Come on Bets, aren't you ready?" Corky called impatiently.

"Hurry yourself! Your mutt and Granny's loused up the party."

"Heap big difference," Corky muttered.

She ran down the backstairs, picked up a bar of soap, grabbed a large basin, and hurried out to the garage. I wasn't far behind.

Corky parked the basin on the floor. "I could spit," she exclaimed.

I did and it made me feel much better. I grabbed two clothes pins, handed one to Corky, and stuck the other on my nose.

Bitzel was our first victim. Corky grasped the squirming dachsy by the collar and half persuaded and half pulled her to the basin. "Into the tub with you," she murmured as she parked her in the water. "Bet you'll think twice about rolling in 'cow' before you do it the next time."

Schnitzel was next. The old lady really gave us a hard time. "It's not my fault," I kept telling her as she struggled to get out of the water. "Who asked you to roll?"

Mom entered. "I'll give you a hand," she volunteered. Mom was dressed in jeans and sounded in the best of temper. Had she forgotten already?

"We're nearly finished." Corky pulled the clothes pin off her nose, stood up, and shook herself. "I'm as wet as the dogs."

"Here's a towel. Dry yourselves quickly and

come to the house. I'll light the fire in the parlor. If we're not careful, you'll all be sick."

The house was wonderfully quiet. All the guests had left and our cleaning lady was fast getting the place back in shape. Large wet spots were all that remained of the cattle smears and with luck they would dry and disappear. The furniture was back where it belonged, the ash trays clean and the cake crumbs swept away.

Mom had lit the fire and we collapsed in front of it. A little warmth felt mighty good. I stared into the fire, fascinated by the crackling flames. The dogs, well-toasted by the blaze, soon were asleep.

"That was quite an afternoon." Mom sank into the leather chair, lit a cigaret and glanced around the room. She looked first at us and then at the dogs. Slowly she started to smile. "I'm sorry I yelled at you kids, but the dachshunds did give me quite a start."

"They spoiled your party!"

"Not really. The tea was almost over," she laughed, "but they did create quite a stir."

"Then you aren't mad?"

"Of course not." Mom came over and hugged us both.

"How about toasting some marshmallows?" Corky always thought about food, and at a time like this!

"Sure thing! Corky, you find the marshmallows. Betsy, you look for a long fork. I'll be the guest." Mom settled contentedly in the chair. "We can relax now. There's nothing special on the program for weeks."

"Oh yes there is!" Corky beamed as she handed Mom a warm, drippy marshmallow.

"Next Sunday's the pet show!"

Chapter 5

The late autumn sun was streaming into my room as I slowly turned over in bed. Five more minutes and then I'd get up.

Schnitzel was sleeping peacefully. She had started to snore of late, but when she became too bad I'd give her a push and she'd roll over.

"People and dogs are much alike," Mom had told me. "If they lie on their backs, they'll snore. Just roll them over and they'll sleep quietly." She should know, Dad is a pretty good snorer.

NO LOVE FOR SCHNITZEL

My alarm went off. It was seven-thirty. I crawled out of bed and banged at Corky's door. "Time to get up lazy," I shouted. "We've got work to do for the pet show."

I brushed my teeth and glanced in the mirror. "Stop blinking," I told myself. I always blinked when I was excited and the pet show had me in a tizzy. Imagine me at a pet show!

My jeans were handy and I slipped into them. Later I'd wear my suit and look respectable, but for now working clothes were by far the best.

Corky and I spread newspaper on the floor, called the dogs, and curried them until their coats shone and the skin beneath rippled. Schnitzel and Bitzel loved the attention and stood quietly while we worked over them. Every time I hit a particularly ticklish spot, Schnitzel's left foot pawed the ground.

"That's a reflex," Corky explained knowingly.

Ear cleaning came next, but that wasn't popular. As soon as Bitzel saw the box of Q-Tips, she dived under my bed. Schnitzel pulled a "me-too" and there we were—dogless.

Corky tried her best to persuade the dachshunds to come out. First she coaxed, then threatened and finally grabbed. "Got you!" she yelled triumphantly as she backed out from under the bed, grasping Bitsy firmly by the collar. Bitsy tried to pull away and nearly choked herself. Luckily Dad came to the rescue. He picked Bitsy up, sat her on his lap, and cleaned out her ears.

"Let's have Schnitzel," he said, putting Bitzel on the ground and patting her on the rump. "You girls are making a big production out of nothing."

Schnitzel had followed Bitzel out from under the bed and I had no difficulty in catching her. I parked her on Dad's knee and swabbed out her ears.

Corky pulled the new green collars and leashes out of the closet and the dachshunds were set to go.

We changed quickly and walked down to Mrs. Ripley's field where the pet show was to be held. Admission was $1.00 per class and the proceeds would go to the American Society for Prevention of Cruelty to Animals. Dad staked us $5.00 worth, and we were on our own.

"Corky, what happens at a pet show?" I inquired. "Will it be mobbed with dogs?"

"Hope so! Mrs. Ripley wants to make pots of money and she'll need a large entry."

I had gotten used to Schnitzel, and since she had been around, the big dogs had bothered me less, but I didn't like the thought of dozens of dogs barking at me. "They aren't running around loose, are they?" I hoped my voice didn't sound as timid as I felt. If I could have, I would have turned Schnitzel over to Corky and headed for home.

"Of course not! Bets, pull yourself together. You'll have a swell time. You might even win a prize."

"Fat chance!"

Schnitzel was leash broken and walked on my left minding her own business. She paid little attention to the string of cars heading for the show. There were station wagons with dog crates, sedans with dignified Great Danes sitting beside their

drivers, and Volkswagen buses loaded with scream-
ing children. Mrs. Ripley would have her fill of
entries.

We arrived at the gate, bought a program for
a quarter, and entered the show grounds. To our
left was the refreshment stand, to our right a red
and white checkered booth operated by a dog
food company. There were dozens of dogs: large,
small, long-haired, short-haired, purebred, and mongrels. Cats of all sizes and descriptions, tortoises,
rabbits, and ducks, and in the far corners of the
field, ponies and donkeys . . . they were giving 25¢
rides and business appeared brisk.

In the center of the field, in a carefully roped
off ring, a tweedy lady and a pipe-smoking gentle-
man were judging the first class. It was for the
smallest dog and they were weighing and measuring a Chihuahua and a toy pug. The Chihuahua
won hands down and received a blue rosette as well
as a five-pound bag of dog chow. "That will last
him a life-time, if they dared feed it to him. Bet

he lives on chicken and tidbits of beef." Corky snorted, "Who'd want a fancy character like that?"

"But he's so nice and small."

"You can have him." She turned to Bitzel. "Let's go and look at some real dogs. We have half an hour before our first class."

Schnitzel and I trailed after her. I didn't want to go, but neither did I want to stay alone. Corky was in no rush. Even she had never seen so many different breeds, and she enjoyed looking them over.

The dogs were anchored to dog boxes, children or cars, and you could walk by them without getting too close. Schnitzel loved it. She trotted along the rows like a general inspecting his troops: her eyes alert, her tail waving in the breeze. She looked them all over critically. Only a great dane caught her fancy. He was huge and looked ferocious, but Schnitzel wished to make his acquaintance. "He'd finish you in one bite," I scolded her, pulling her away and hurrying after Corky.

She was standing in front of a small pekinese admiring his pug nose and his long soft coat. "Isn't he a doll!"

He had short legs and poppy eyes, but his fur was gorgeous. "He sure is." Anything was better than the great dane Schnitzel had tried to introduce me to.

I bent down to pet him, but without as much as a growl he grabbed my hand and hung onto it.

I yelled. His owner whacked him and he let go. Luckily for me, his teeth weren't very sharp and he didn't break the skin.

"That'll teach you not to pet little dogs. They're usually the meanest!" Corky pulled me away. She looked as upset as I felt.

The peke's owner came running after us. "Are you all right, dear?" She looked at my hand. "Poor Saito was just trying to be friendly. He doesn't know his own strength."

Corky took my arm and the four of us walked away.

My hand didn't hurt much, but I felt like cry-ing. "I'm going home Corks. I don't like pet shows."

"Can't blame you, but . . ." she looked first at me, and then at Schnitzel, "how about staying for one class? the dog with the longest tail is coming up now, and Schnitzel is entered."

I shook my head and sniffed.

"Be a sport! Dad isn't going to think much of you if you come home with your tail between your legs." Corky always used dog language when she tried to be extra persuasive.

"I'll stay for this class. But then I'm off." I blew my nose, buttoned my jacket, dusted Schnitzel with my Kleenex, and followed Corky into the ring.

There were twenty entries: Irish setters, pointers, collies, police dogs and dachshunds paraded around with their owners. We circled the field twice and then lined up in the center.

The judges moved up and down the line, measuring every tail. One used a yardstick, while the other wrote the results down in his book.

The dogs didn't enjoy having their tails measured and tucked them between their legs, or even sat on them.

Bitzel's turn came first. Corky stood her up in real show style: her head alert and her tail stretched out behind her.

The judge looked approvingly. "You make it easy for us," she said with a smile. But however hard Corky tried, Bitzel's tail only measured nine inches.

We came next, but Schnitzel first wagged her tail and wiggled her rump, and then sat down and looked at me with a puzzled expression.

The judge laughed, "It's a shame to worry a nice, old person like that. Hold her still and I'll measure her."

Eight inches was the best that we could do.

I petted Schnitzel and sat down on the grass. She was panting. I loosened her collar, fondled her ears absentmindedly, and kept my eye on the judges. They had finished measuring. It wouldn't be long before they'd announce the results.

I got up to listen, whistled to Schnitzel, and

walked ahead. But the opposite direction looked more attractive to her. "Don't you want to hear?" I said crossly and gave her a little yank. That was all she needed. She slipped her collar and was off.

"Schnitzel come here!"

She turned and looked, wagged her tail knowingly, and bustled away.

"Schnitzel come here immediately!" Corky commanded but the determined little dog paid no attention.

"She's got something on her mind." Corky was fascinated.

"She isn't running away, she's heading for a definite place. We'd better she what she's up to."

I had no choice, and for the second time that day, I trailed after Corky and Bitzel.

I might have known, Schnitzel headed straight for the great dane. "She'll be eaten alive," I wailed.

"We'll grab her first."

But we didn't. She was still out of our reach when she arrived at the great dane's lair. "That's the one she wanted to talk with before."

"Heap big difference." Corky was noticeably upset.

Schnitzel wagged her tail, walked right up to him, licked his nose, and parked herself between his front paws.

The enormous beast looked surprised. Like a cat playing with a mouse, he put one huge paw on Schnitzel's back and lowered his head.

"He's going to kill her," I screamed. "Corky do something!" But Corky was glued to the ground. Without thinking, I rushed in and tried to grab Schnitzel, but I tripped over the dane's rope and fell flat on my face in front of him.

He sat up with a start, looked at both of us, then ignored me, and licked Schnitzel from top to toe.

I pulled myself together and gingerly put the collar around Schnitzel's neck, but she was in no hurry to move. Without thinking, I patted the big beast. He licked my hand. He was so big and yet so friendly.

"Come on Schnitzel old girl," I said gently.

"It's time to go." I gathered up my dog, slipped her lead on and walked home. I was glad to be alone. I had so much to think about. What had this little dog done to me? I was petrified of the great dane, but I had plunged in to rescue her. It made me proud. For once, I was the heroine instead of Corky.

I put my hands in my pocket and walked faster. It was cold, but I felt wonderful. Schnitzel, too, enjoyed the brisk fall day. It was good fun to have a dog, to take it for walks, and to pet shows. As for my room, it really didn't suffer much. On the whole, Schnitzel was pretty clean. Would Mom let me take her to South Carolina for Christmas? That would really be great! Corky'd have Bitsy and I'd have a dog of my own.

Chapter 6

Eight suitcases, three guns, four fishing rods, Mom, Dad, Corky, the dachshunds, and myself joined the milling mobs at Pennsylvania Station. It was December twenty-third and we were on our way to Grandma's house in South Carolina.

Omar, that's what we called Dad's mother, and Grandpa moved south after he retired. Gramps loved to hunt and Omar liked the mild South Carolina winters. She talked about how run down the place was, but Grandpa had let her do over the house. She learned to like it so well that after his death she remained there alone. For us, Christmas at "Horton Hill" was the high point of the winter.

As usual, our train was late and the station was teeming with holiday travellers. The dogs hated the crowds and the shrill railroad noises. They shivered, stuck close to Corky and me, and gave us that, "Why did you bring us here?" look.

"Go buy some funnies and walk your dogs. Fidgeting won't get you any place," said Dad, pulling a handful of coins out of his pocket. He was grumpy today, but he'd been working real hard and was tired. It would all be different in South Carolina.

"Don't walk too far, the train may be announced at any time." Mom was a nervous traveller.

We wandered off into the main part of the station, bought our comics, and studied the machines, selling apples, sandwiches, and ice cream.

"Too bad we spent so much on funnies. I'd love to try one of those ice cream sticks." Corky looked back at the machine longingly. "I adore ice cream."

"We'll have it for supper tonight." I didn't care that much about food, but dinner on the train was fun.

"West Coast Champion now boarding on track eight," boomed over the loudspeaker.

We hurried back and helped the red cap load our bags onto the truck. Mom counted the pieces and we were off.

"I'll carry Schnitzel, she's far too heavy for you." Dad scooped her up in his arms and followed our baggage into the elevator. Corky grabbed Bitzel. She was heavy, squirmy, and difficult to carry. "You're going on a diet tomorrow," Corky mumbled threateningly, "or the next time, you can walk yourself onto the train."

We found car A121 and soon made ourselves comfortable. Mom and Dad shared one compartment, Corky, the dogs, and I, the other. The porter opened the door between and we were ready to go. We studied our comics, Mom and Dad read, and the dogs slept on the seat. But I wasn't looking forward to tonight. I didn't want a dachshund messing up my new pajamas. As dogs go, Schnitzel was pretty good, but she did snore and scratch and sometimes she even smelled. Corky enjoyed Bitsy on her bed, but I'd never get used to that. Whether Schnitzel liked it or not, tonight the floor would have to do.

The train rumbled on. Newark went by, then Princeton Junction, and finally Philadelphia. "Watch for the zoo," Corky instructed me. "It'll be coming soon."

"It's dead ahead," Mom shouted from the other room.

The Philadelphia Zoo was one of our landmarks. The trip would not have been the same without it.

Corky woke Bitzel and made her look out of the window. "You want to see the elephants, don't you?" she asked her long-eared friend.

"Don't think she cares." I wasn't going to start that kind of nonsense with Schnitzel.

NO LOVE FOR SCHNITZEL

The elephant house, the lions' lair, and the seals' pool flashed by in quick succession. Bitsy's moist nose smeared up the window, but she was sleepy. As soon as Corky let her, she left her window seat, collapsed back into her chair, and was dreaming in no time.

The train rumbled on. I pulled out my animal coloring book and worked on some handsome dogs. Corky was filling in the blanks of a crossword puzzle, but her heart wasn't in it. She chewed her pencil, looked out of the window, and ambled up and down the hall.

"You look bored." Dad knew us pretty well.

"Sort of. How about going to the dining car?" she suggested hopefully. "Isn't it nearly dinner time?"

Mom looked at her watch. "Not really," she said with a smile, "but let's go anyway. It'll keep you both occupied. By eating early, we might avoid a waiting line."

At home it's no fun cleaning up for dinner. But here the wash basin pulled down from the wall and if I pushed the right lever, hot or cold water spurted into the shiny metal basin. The soap was little and wrapped in paper, the towels had Pullman Company written all over them, and the mirror was full of me. Straighten out your wiggly part, it warned me, or your mother will complain. As for Omar, she'll call you a paleface. There hadn't been much sun in Connecticut lately. Even my freckles had disappeared, but a few days in South Carolina would fix that.

Corky filled a paper cup and brought it to the dogs. "Wet your tongue, Bitzel," she said "but don't drink too much, it'll just make you uncomfortable."

Bitzel lapped up half, and Schnitzel emptied the cup. We petted the dogs, closed the door carefully, and headed for the diner.

Dad went first, then Mom, and Corky and I brought up the rear. The train swayed and so did we—through Pullman cars with compartments in the front and roomettes the rest of the way. We stopped to look at one. "Roomettes are neat," Corky explained. "The chair makes up into a bed, but . . ." she began to giggle. "If you want to use the john, you have to push the bed up. Very difficult if you're sharing it with your dog."

By the time we reached the diner, six cars away, I still hadn't figured out how it could be done.

"Listen to Corky and you'll never starve," Dad kidded her. He didn't like eating early, but he preferred anything to waiting in line.

A big waiter dressed in white brought up the menu, but we already knew what we wanted: chicken in the basket for us and steaks for Mom and Pop.

A single red carnation shook in the bud vase, the silver rattled on the table, and the water, like breakers on a beach, pounded the sides of the carafe. Our train was making time through the dark Maryland landscape.

"Look at that portion!" Mom exclaimed in mock horror as the waiter set a basket of fried chicken and corn fritters in front of me. "Bet you can't eat half!"

Corky kicked me under the table. "Oh sure she can," she answered brightly. "She's a big girl now."

"Eat what you like and we'll bring the rest to the dogs," she whispered.

The chicken was great, the fritters crunchy and the cranberry jelly delicious. Eating was fun when it tasted this good.

Corky attacked hers in a most businesslike manner: one bite of chicken, then a piece of fritter and the cranberry sauce for a chaser. Suddenly the train gave a lurch. Corky's chicken, fritters and all, slipped slowly off the plate onto her lap. I gasped, Mom and Dad looked surprised, but Corky took it in stride. The food landed on her napkin and without a break in the conversation, she carefully flipped it back onto her plate.

We'd just about finished when we neared Washington. "Let's hurry and air the dogs. We'll be here for at least a half hour." Corky was all set to go.

"Do you think they should?" Mom liked to keep her brood together.

"It won't do much for the dogs, but it will be good for the kids. Write down the car, train, and platform number and be back in fifteen minutes. After that, the train will be shifted to another platform and you might have trouble finding us."

We grabbed our bag of leftovers and dashed to our compartment. Corky took the chicken and the fritters, and fed them to the dogs. "That's too much. They'll get sick!" I knew that dogs were supposed to be fed little while travelling.

"Don't be such a stinker. Why should we be the only ones to have a good dinner? Dogs like to eat too." Corky sounded most convincing.

I shrugged my shoulders, tightened Schnitzel's collar, and followed Corky out onto the platform.

The dogs were delighted to be back with us and paid little attention to the crowds. They walked along sniffing at an ice wagon here and a luggage truck there. But they had no intention of attending to business. They were used to grass, and there was no similarity between it and a cement platform.

We walked out to the large, circular information desk and to the news stand where Corky bought a candy bar.

"Aren't you stuffed?" I inquired.

"Sure," she admitted, "but we might get hungry later."

"Don't you think we should head back?" I was beginning to feel nervous.

"No rush. We have loads of time." If Corky didn't want to be hurried, there was little I could do about it.

Finally she glanced at the large station clock and was surprised at the time. "I guess we'd better step on it, or Mom and Dad will start to worry."

At that moment the chicken and the greasy fritters got the better of Schnitzel. The poor dog was miserable. Bitsy was fine. She was much younger and nothing ever bothered her.

"It's all your fault!" I was furious at Corky. "You shouldn't have given her that rich food!"

Corky said little. She knew we couldn't move the old dog and it was getting later and later. Finally

TRACK
38

Schnitzel perked up and we dashed for the train.

Corky ran and Schnitzel and I had trouble keeping up. We made it back to platform eight, but our train was nowhere to be seen.

"Darn it! It's moved already."

"How'll we find it?"

"We'll ask. We do speak English, you know." When Corky worried, she always took it out on me.

There was no one to question so we tore back to the information desk. It was mobbed. We went to the shortest line and tried to wait our turn. The line didn't move, but the clock did. "We're going to miss our train!" I started to cry.

The lady in front of us turned around. "What is it little girl?"

"We're going to miss our train," I wailed.

"We'll be all right if we can just find out what platform it's on," Corky spoke up.

"What train are you looking for?" The information man must have heard us.

"The West Coast Champion," Corky shouted.

"Platform fifteen, and hurry. It's due to pull out in two minutes."

"Come on, Schnitzel," I yelled. The little dog wagged her tail knowingly and galloped alongside. She was old and fat, and a little under the weather, but when the chips were down she could keep up with all of us.

Dad met us at the gate. He was frantic. "Where in the blazes have you been? We've been looking all over for you." He picked up the dogs and pushed us onto the train.

"All aboard," the conductor yelled and the West Coast Champion pulled out of Washington Station. What a narrow squeak. Corky was far too adventurous for me.

"Time for bed, kids." Mom didn't say much about our Washington escapade, but I knew she'd been terribly scared.

The porter had made up our berths during the Washington stop-over and we undressed quickly.

"Raise your shades. The Capitol is on our left," Dad's voice boomed from the adjoining room. We ran over to the window and stared. It was like fairyland. The dome was brighter than day and sparkled, and so did the tall column of the Washington Monument. The rest of the city was black, interspersed with thousands of brightly lit houses and broad sweeps of illuminated highways. The train rumbled on, Washington was behind us and the quiet Virginia countryside lay ahead.

I was going to make Corky toss for the lower, but it was my turn to take the upper, and tonight of all nights I wasn't going to make a fuss. I put my suitcase neatly under my bed and, holding my book, climbed into the upper berth. The ladder was rocky, but I made it. I turned on the reading light and started my book.

Corky was impressed. She looked up at me and grinned. "What, no argument. Are you feeling all right?" She dug into her suitcase and handed me a piece of candy. Corky put Bitzel's blanket on her bed, deposited her on top of it, and turned out the center light.

Mom came and kissed us goodnight. She climbed

halfway up the ladder and tucked me in. "Don't worry about Schnitzel, I'll take care of her. She can sleep on my bed."

"That's swell!" I snuggled down in the bed. It was warm and comfortable. Tomorrow we'd be in South Carolina for Christmas at Horton Hill. I shut my eyes. Would Schnitzel like her Christmas present? It was a big surprise. No one knew about it— not even Corky.

Chapter 7

My cousin, Geoff, met us at the railroad station. He was tall, thin and wonderful, could drive a car, shoot and ride. But an upper middler at Exeter had little use for an eleven-year-old girl cousin. He probably thought I was a scrawny, brown-haired kid with green cat's eyes. I wasn't allowed to shoot and I can't ride very well, but someday I might. Mom always said, "You can do anything you set your mind on."

He didn't pay much attention to Corky either,

but whenever he was around she would spruce up, and Dad never had to tell her, "Corky, you're looking like an unmade bed." Geoff's parents were stationed overseas and he spent all his vacations with Omar.

We walked the dogs behind the station and then piled into the car for the ten mile trip to Omar's house. I always liked this drive. The road, flanked by miles and miles of pine woods, was straight and little used. Occasionally we'd see a tumbledown house or a wooden church or a field of Bermuda grass, now brown and crinkled with cold. It was early morning, but even in December the sky was turning deep blue. Only the wintry fields looked dull and tired.

Bitsy took in all the sights. She sat on Corky's lap, her nose pressed against the glass, studying the scenery. Once in a while she'd yelp joyfully, as if she'd remembered that particular spot and the fun we'd had there. Schnitzel slept on. The pine woods meant nothing to her.

A short half hour later we arrived at Horton

Hill. Omar had heard the car coming up the drive and was on the porch to meet us. She was small and sturdy. Her cheeks were rosy and weather-beaten, her short gray hair windblown and her eyes, like my father's, deep blue and piercing. She looked young in an oldish sort of way. I hugged her. "Who's your friend?" she inquired, pointing to my four-legged sausage.

"That's my dog, Schnitzel, and she's a wonder-ful girl. She came all the way from home without misbehaving."

"That's very impressive," Omar laughed. "But how about letting them run now. Don't you think they need a little exercise?"

We helped with the luggage, said "Hello" to Lyda, the cook, and dashed to our rooms. The Christmas decorations weren't up yet. Omar always saved that job for us, but somehow the whole place smelt "Christmasy." Lyda must be baking. It wouldn't be long before we'd be sampling her cookies.

We unpacked. Dad took charge of the guns and fishing gear and then we had lunch.

"We'll decorate the house this afternoon," Omar announced over dessert. I've collected evergreens, holly and ribbons. . . ."

"How about the mistletoe?" Geoff interrupted.

"That's your job. I know you enjoy shooting it down."

"May I go along?" Corky butted in.

"How about me?" I wasn't going to be left out of everything.

"We need you Bets. Omar and I can't manage alone."

Mom was being politic, but I knew that the big kids didn't want me. I'd never been mistletoe shooting and I thought it would be fun. The white berries grow in bunches at the top of cyprus trees. You either climb up after them or shoot them down. Shooting is easier and much safer.

"You be a good girl, Bets, and I'll take you dove shooting." Geoff knew how disappointed I must be.

I looked at him gratefully and finished my apple pie in silence.

The moment lunch was over, Dad headed for

the gun room and Corky and Geoff fetched the jeep. "Hurry back with the mistletoe," I called after them. "We'll be ready for it." I wasn't going to let them know how much I wanted to go along.

The tree was first. A large cedar had been cut and was waiting for us in the living room. Mom and I fetched boxes and boxes of Christmas trimmings from the attic and carted them downstairs.

We sorted our treasures and divvied up the job. Mom worked on the top of the tree and I trimmed the bottom. We covered the cedar with silver bells, shiny blue balls, painted pine cones, and cornucopias filled with candy. Mom fixed the star at the top and the lights, and both of us draped the tree's branches with angel hair and covered the base with greens.

We sat back and admired our handiwork. "Pretty handsome, if I say so myself." Mom was pleased.

Schnitzel, sniffing around, tracked down the candy. But I'd been smart. I'd hung it out of reach. "Here Schnitzel," I called and fed her some left over chocolate nuts. Schnitzel eyed the little pellets suspiciously, tried hard to chew them, and finally swallowed them in one gulp. She licked her chops and looked for more.

"Want some, Ma?" I offered the bag.

"No thank you, Bets. I'll get fat. You're the only one who can eat what you please; but nothing much pleases you."

"Oh yes it does. I like candy." I stuck the rest of the bag in my pocket and followed her into the dining room to see what Omar was up to.

We must have taken more time than we thought, for Omar had been up to a lot. The front hall was gay with large vases of red berries, and ropes of ground pine covered the banister. In the dining room my grandmother's favorite white bowl was filled with holly, and Omar, perched on a step ladder, was putting the finishing touches to garlands of bay leaves.

"Here let me help you," Mom ran over. "Why don't you stay on the ground and let the young fry do the climbing?"

"I suppose I should, but I bet I'm better at it than they are." And to prove it, Granny reached for a particularly stubborn bough.

"Probably," Mom laughed, "but . . ."

The door banged and Corky, Bitzel, and Geoff were back, loaded with mistletoe.

"The shooting must have been good."

"It sure was. Geoff let me use his gun." Corky breathless with excitement pointed to a small bunch she was carrying.

"Geoff let you shoot?" I was green.

"Once." Corky knew she had talked out of turn. She wasn't supposed to handle a gun unless a grown-up was along.

Mom made no comment, but she had that "I'll see you later," expression on her face.

Omar noticed nothing wrong. "That's swell kids," she said, delighted with their loot. "Put it all in the pantry."

We did, and then I headed for the kitchen. Cooking would be much more fun than messing around with mistletoe. They'd shot it down. Let them figure out where to put it.

The kitchen was warm and steamy and smelled delicious as Lyda put the last batch of fruit cake into the black coal oven.

"Want some, Honey?" said she offering me a slice.

"Sure thing." I stuck a piece in my mouth. Corky wouldn't get any. She was always on a diet when Geoff was around and stayed out of the kitchen.

I prowled around examining all the goodies. "It looks as if the baking's all finished." I must have sounded disappointed.

"It is, but I need you to fix the cookie trays. The carol sing is tonight."

On Christmas eve around six o'clock all the neighboring colored folk came to sing Christmas carols. There were always dozens of little ones, and it was Corky's and my job to pass the refreshments.

Arranging cookies wasn't as good as mixing

batter, chopping nuts, and melting chocolate, but it did have its advantages. Lyda didn't care how many I ate and Schnitzel cleaned up the crumbs. Omar's setters wandered in for an occasional handout, and although they rubbed against my legs, I didn't mind them too much. I was far too busy.

I decorated the trays with Christmas paper and sprigs of holly, and loaded them with sugared stars, iced Christmas trees, and Santa Clauses.

Lyda, her hands on her ample hips, admired my artistry. "That's fine, Bets," she chuckled, "but I'd better disappear them if I want some left for the carol sing."

"I think I'll go and help Dad get ready!" Dad was to be Santa Claus. He pretended to object to being stuffed into the antique red suit, but I really think he liked it.

"Don't stab me, Bets," he'd yell as I safety pinned the suit around his neck.

As for Corky, this was her one time to get even. She looked at him critically and said, "You don't

80

need a pillow this year, you're round enough without it."

Mom came to Dad's rescue. She gave our handiwork a final check and adjusted his bewhiskered mask. "Santa isn't going to be much use if he can't see."

Omar had little gifts for all the visitors who came to the carol sing. These Corky and I loaded into a toy cart for Dad to distribute.

"I'll hide the wagon in the coat room," I volunteered, and when Corky joined the family in the living room, I tucked Schnitzel's present in the bottom of the cart. It had her name on it, and just thinking about it made me feel warm all over.

We had spent Christmas this way for as long as I could remember, but this year it was special. There was one more dog in the house, my own dog, and I had remembered to buy her a Christmas present. At Horton Hill, as at home, the dogs were privileged characters, but none of them received presents—not even Bitzel.

NO LOVE FOR SCHNITZEL

We gathered around the tree in the living room. It glittered with blue and silver lights and cast a warm glow over the entire room as Omar greeted her guests.

The colored folks, dressed in their Sunday best, wished her the joys of the season. Dozens of little kids, wide eyed with excitement, waited for Santa. At the stroke of six the plantation bell rang and Santa appeared pulling his cart. As he neared the tree we welcomed him with, "Here comes Santa Claus!"

The dachshunds with big red ribbons tied around their collars were part of the group. They were puzzled by all the commotion and sniffed our guests suspiciously.

Omar sat in her chair and the rest of us stood around while Dad asked the usual questions. "Have you been good boys and girls?" he inquired in a deep booming voice, but he never waited for an answer.

Geoff was his assistant, and whenever Dad couldn't read the name on the package, he'd translate. Finally, Geoff came to a small lumpy package. He did a double take and read, "To Schnitzel from Betsy."

Corky looked up. I could almost hear her say, "Why didn't I think of buying a present for my dog?"

I called Schnitzel, unwrapped the present and handed it to her. It was a rubber dog angel, complete with squeaker, and it had cost me one dollar and seventy-nine cents. Schnitzel sniffed politely, wagged her tail and wandered off toward Bitsy and the tree. My first doggy Christmas present was a flop!

I wanted to cry, but I couldn't let everybody see how I felt. I'd tried so hard to be kind to Schnitzel, and she didn't give a hoot. It would be a long time before I'd spend a month's pocket money on her again!

"That's a darling toy." Mom comforted me. "Schnitzel will love to play with it later. There's just too much excitement now."

When the last package was gone, Pete, the

oldest retainer on Horton Hill, signaled to Lyda and to their kinfolk and soon the room reverberated with old favorites; "Remember Me," "Silent Night," and "Away in a Manger." Then Peter cleared his throat. It was his privilege to tell the wonderful story of the birth of the Christ Child.

At that moment little Annabelle started to giggle. Her elders tried to hush her up, but soon all the small ones joined in. Corky and I looked in their direction and saw Bitzel and Schnitzel each carrying off a cornucopia filled with candy. They had purposely been hung high up, and how they ever reached them I'll never know. But two warriors of old couldn't have been prouder of their spoils.

We gave chase, but they outran us, their ears flapping and their short legs hot footing it out of the house.

"Let them go!" Corky grabbed my arm. She was breathless. "Let them have their fun. If that's their idea of a Christmas treat. Why stop them?"

NO LOVE FOR SCHNITZEL

We returned to the living room. Pete had finished and it was time to serve refreshments.

When my last cookie had disappeared, I called my candy hound and again showed her her present. This time she was interested. I threw it; she gave chase, squeaked it a couple of times and brought it back for a repeat performance. Once she caught on, she didn't want to stop. Finally I was tired. I sat down on the floor and she lay down next to me.

What a wonderful day it had been. I stroked her head and ears, leaned against a chair and shut my eyes. Schnitzel tucked the angel between her front paws, placed her head on top of it and snored gently.

Tomorrow we'd go to early church, open our own presents, and eat Lyda's whopping turkey dinner. And the day after that, we'd dove shoot. I petted my dog. "Have a good sleep," I whispered in her ear, "and save your strength. You'll need it."

Chapter 8

"I'm sorry Corky, but your Mother says no."
The voices in the gun room were loud.

"I'll go to bed right after the dove shoot,"
Corky pleaded with Father.

"No one is trying to punish you, but a corn
field in December is no place for a bad cold."

So that's what it was all about. Corky had de-
veloped a sore throat on Christmas day, and by this
morning her nose was a mess.

The door opened and my sister, red-eyed and

weeping, dashed upstairs. Not being invited to watch Geoff shoot mistletoe was mild compared with staying in bed while the whole neighborhood went dove shooting.

The Christmas shoot at Horton Hill was famous. Dad organized the shoot and afterwards everyone came back to the house for drinks. It was as much a part of Christmas at Omar's as the carol sing or Lyda's turkey.

"Step on it, Bets," Geoff called to me from the porch, "if you and your great retriever want to go with me." He hadn't forgotten his promise.

"Just one sec!" I yelled delightedly. I rushed upstairs, grabbed my windbreaker, stuck my new red scarf in the pocket, and whistled to Schnitzel. Poor Corky. I picked up the dog angel and a box of candy Lyda had given me and knocked on her door.

Muffled sobs were my only answer.

I found Corky sprawled on the bed, her head buried in Bitsy's side. She must have heard me, but didn't look up. For a moment I stood at the door awkwardly, then I pushed the box of candy and the dog angel into her hand.

"Here's something for you and Bitzel," I stammered. And before she could answer, I was down the stairs and out of the house.

The jeep was at the door with Geoff in the driver's seat. Dad stood nearby in an old pair of shooting pants and a coat, with a game bag slung over his shoulder and a guest list in his hand. Only his velour hat with feathered band was new. Mom had given it to him for Christmas and this was its first outing.

As each gunner drove in, Dad told him where to go: the sycamore tree, Watson's old house, clay pipes, and the tractor shed were some of the stations.

There were twenty-five men. Dove shooting is one of the few games where more rather than less gunners make for better sport. Guns are stationed around the edges of all the fields. As the birds come in for their afternoon meal they are shot at and so fly to another field.

NO LOVE FOR SCHNITZEL

Most of the hunters knew the landmarks. The few that were strangers climbed into the jeep for us to deliver.

"We're off!" yelled Geoff as he put the jeep in gear. There were six of us. Three in the front: Geoff, Mr. Jones, the fat druggist, and me squashed between them, my legs curled around the gear shift. On top of the dog box perched three more visitors, their guns firmly placed in the gun racks. And in the dog box, built to hold six pointers, sat Schnitzel.

We drove along the back road. Pine woods surrounded us and directly ahead lay a ribbon of pale sand, the road that was to take us to the dove fields.

"First stop, Watson's old house," Geoff sang out as he brought the jeep to a grinding halt.

The fat druggist piled out and nearly stepped on a piglet scurrying for cover. Mr. Jones swore and inched forward with care. He stationed himself, complete with two boxes of extra shells and a stool to sit on, overlooking the first corn field.

"Jones may have the choice spot," Geoff mumbled enviously as the jeep started up. The sand on the road became heavier and we skidded rather than drove.

"Do you think Schnitzel's all right?" I asked. "She's old, you know!"

"Sure. There's plenty of straw in the box and a little bouncing will be good for her liver." Geoff grinned.

After we had dropped our last passenger we drove to the farthest field, our spot for the afternoon. Geoff parked the jeep out of sight, picked up his shot gun, and stuffed his pockets with shells. Then, lifting Schnitzel out of the box, he petted the old dog, pulled her ears gently, and handed her to me.

The sky was gray and the wind was picking up. I shivered a little as Schnitzel and I followed Geoff around the edge of the woods. He signaled to me. We backed out of sight and waited. The field looked bleak and uninviting; bare brown ploughed ground, interspersed with frozen corn stalks. If I were a dove, I'd find better pickings elsewhere.

NO LOVE FOR SCHNITZEL

I tied my red wooly scarf firmly around my head, stuck my hands in my pockets, and leaned against the nearest tree. Schnitzel snuffled around and appeared interested.

Suddenly at a distance a shot rang out, then another, and another.

"Hark," shouted Geoff and we both scanned the sky. If they were shooting in the other fields, the birds should start to fly our way.

"Over there," I yelled pointing to three doves flying high, but toward us.

"They're out of range, but keep watching."

The shooting continued and birds flew all about us. They were gray, graceful and fast. Wind puffs buffeted them, but whenever they neared us they veered off.

"Stay here!" Geoff ordered and carefully walked to the corner. Soon the field was alive with birds. The doves came in twos and threes.

Geoff's first shot was a beauty and the bird dropped in front of him. His second missed and his third was a long one. The bird was hit, but it headed toward the pine woods and would be hard to find.

Should Schnitzel and I try to retrieve or should we stay put?

Orders are orders, but I was cold and bored. I dashed out onto the field, picked up the bird that had dropped near Geoff and handed it to him. But when I appeared, the doves veered away.

"Take that red scarf off and get back into the trees!" Geoff's words stopped me short. I tore off my beautiful Christmas present and slunk back to the woods' edge. I'd loused up his shooting. He would never take me again.

Geoff strode on without a word and Schnitzel and I were quite alone. "Might as well go back to the jeep. It'll be warmer. Some dove shoot," I grumbled to myself. "Corky isn't missing a thing."

Schnitzel was enjoying herself. She had helped herself to the dove I had picked up and took turns worrying it and then guarding it. For the lack of something better to do, I threw it for her. She dashed after it and swallowed a mouthful of feathers, but with a little persuasion she returned it to me. "That's a good girl!" I petted her, picked the remaining feathers from her mouth and threw it again. Schnitzel bounded after it, retrieved and proudly presented it to me. My dog angel practice had paid off.

I decided to find Geoff's long shot. I knew where it had disappeared, but doves are small and hundreds of pines are confusing. I called Schnitzel and walked in the general direction. I showed her our dove and motioned her to fetch. We criss-crossed the area, looking under every stump and tuft of grass. I worked my toe through the scraggly underbrush and Schnitzel used her nose like a gei-ger counter.

Suddenly Schnitzel tensed up. She pointed momentarily and then pounced. A wing beat feebly, then a slight scuffle, and soon my heroine trotted back to me, carrying a very dead dove. I hugged her, kissed her, and stuck the dove in my pocket. Geoff was on the other side and because I didn't dare to cross the field, it would take some time to catch up with him.

We were so proud. I skipped along the edge and Schnitzel strutted like a peacock. "We'll surprise him," I whispered, "and then he'll be pleased that he brought us."

Geoff's back was turned, and in this high wind he couldn't hear us approaching, but I could see that he had a little pile of doves beside him. His afternoon had not been wasted.

Suddenly a barrage of shots rang out. Schnitzel sat up and pricked her ears. Geoff took the safety off his gun and waited. The doves glided our way, windblown and crooked. Geoff aimed at one, led it, and fired. It wavered crazily and dropped. More doves came and Geoff reloaded and fired.

When the first bird fell, I motioned to Schnitzel. She scurried out, picked it up, and brought it to me. Granny had given me a retriever and didn't know it. I was the luckiest girl ever.

Geoff watched in amazement. "That's the best dove retriever I've seen in ages. Who trained her?"

"Me," I answered in a small voice.

Geoff looked impressed. "Sorry I was rough

about your scarf Betsy. Thought you knew that doves don't like anything bright."

"I didn't mean to gum you up."

Geoff laughed. "You and Schnitzel have made up for it."

He bent down and fondled my dog, then he turned to me, bowed very formally, and said, "Will you and Miss Schnitzel do me the honor of accompanying me to all the dove shoots?"

I was speechless with pleasure. I buried my head in Schnitzel's neck. Pull yourself together, you goon. I looked up at Geoff and with as much dignity as I could muster said, "Miss Schnitzel and I shall be delighted."

It was getting late and no more doves were coming in to feed. Laden with birds, we struggled back. I pocketed some, Geoff's coat was bulging, and Schnitzel carried her last retrieve.

We climbed into the jeep. Schnitzel, sitting on my lap, rode home in triumph. As we bumped toward the house, I remembered Mom's words. "You've got to be willing to try," she had said. I hadn't wanted Schnitzel, but now I couldn't do without her. She kept me company, amused me, and even helped me to make a hit with Geoff. I'd have to write Granny and tell her, or better still, soon after our return home, Granny would be visiting and she'd see for herself.

"You'll have to be nice to her," I told Schnitzel as she lay curled up in my lap. "Granny may not have taken you dove shooting, but she loved you very much and for many years gave you a wonderful home."

Chapter 9

"Schnitzel, where are you? Granny's coming and I've got to give you a grooming." We were home again and I couldn't wait to see Mom's mother—I had so much to tell her.

"Get up, you lazy loafer. Don't you want to look beautiful for Granny?" I stood her up like a show dog and brushed her from stem to stern. She tried to wriggle out of my clutches, but I held fast.

I brushed and brushed. Schnitzel yawned with boredom. "Is all this fuss necessary?" she seemed to say.

I tied a bright red ribbon around her neck, patted her bottom, and let her go.

She shook herself, scratched at the ribbon, and trotted into the hall.

"She's had enough," Corky called from her room. "She doesn't like being spruced up any more than I do."

A car horn sounded and I dashed downstairs to greet my grandmother. Schnitzel was there ahead of me, barking her lungs out. As soon as the door opened, she flung herself at Granny, and yelped with joy.

"I guess you haven't forgotten me!" Granny picked her up, hugged the old dog, and let the dachshund lick her face.

"Schnitzel, give us a chance."

We kissed Granny, took her coat and suitcase upstairs and helped her unpack.

"I haven't had so much fuss made over me in years," Granny's face beamed. She looked well, but her New York pallor was in sharp contrast to our South Carolina windburns.

Bitzel joined the welcoming committee and the

room was so full of people and dogs that Granny could hardly move.

"All we need are a few Irish setters and then we'll have a real traffic jam," Mom joked.

"I like it. My New York apartment is much too quiet."

Schnitzel dogged Granny's every footstep and even followed her into the bathroom. And I had worried that my dog wouldn't be nice. How silly could I be?

"Time to feed the dogs," Mom called from downstairs.

I whistled to Bitzel and Schnitzel, but only Bitzel followed me to the kitchen. Schnitzel stayed with Granny and pretended not to hear.

"Have it your own way." I mixed Bitzel's meat and beans and gave it to her. "If you're not hungry, Schnitzel, don't eat." I slammed the can opener back into the drawer. I was getting fed up.

Mom watched me with a worried frown on her face. "You should have expected this."

"But does she have to be so obvious about

it?" Grudgingly I picked up Schnitzel's bowl and brought it upstairs. I wasn't going to upset Granny.

Without so much as a "thank you," Schnitzel cleaned it up, licked her chops and parked herself next to Granny.

I went to my room, banged my door, and started my homework. I chewed my pen moodily. I had wanted Schnitzel to be nice to Granny, but I sure hated her to act as if I didn't exist.

I heard everyone go down. Usually I liked an excuse to stop my homework, but this evening I would have much preferred to study.

I gave my red dress a tug. It was getting short, but it was still my favorite. I blew my nose and ambled downstairs.

Dad was fixing a sherry for Granny.

"Hi, Dad."

"Evening, Bets. Would you like some tomato juice?"

"No thanks." I shook my head and glanced at Granny. Sure enough, Schnitzel was sitting on her lap and hadn't bothered to look my way. Ungrateful mutt!

Corky and Bitzel were curled up on the sofa. Dad's setters were sleeping by the fire. I was the only dogless one.

"I'm going out to help Mom," I announced, and hurried to the kitchen.

Mom glanced at me. She looked as if she was going to say something and then changed her mind. "Glad you came out. I can use some help," was her only comment.

The table was set with the red and silver table cloth Granny had given Mom for Christmas. The best china was in use, and there were wine glasses on the table. This was going to be a real party. I cheered up a little. Parties were fun.

"Dinner in five minutes," Mom said. "The roast beef's ready and I'm dishing out the vegetables."

I filled the water glasses, put the rolls and butter on the table, and ran to the parlor to tell them that Mom was all set.

"She's had a great time with your dog," I heard Dad say to Granny as I approached.

"I'm so glad, and I've never seen Schnitzel look better. She wouldn't have liked it in an apartment."

I slowed down. I didn't want to burst in on them.

"I'm happy that Schnitzel remembers me, but I hope it doesn't upset Betsy."

"Now don't you worry. You're not here for long and Betsy will understand."

Dad was right. I was behaving like a dope. It wouldn't hurt me and it was making Granny and Schnitzie happy.

Dinner was swell. Granny was full of jokes, Mom was delighted to have her, and Dad was the perfect host.

He produced a bottle of red wine with a flourish and then served it around the table. He even gave me a little. I felt very grown-up, but the wine tasted terrible.

"Here's to Granny," Dad toasted her.

We all lifted our glasses and drank to her

health. I picked up my wine glass, took a tiny sip, and washed it down with a gulp of water.

"Wine with a water chaser," Corky teased. "When will you ever grow up?"

"Mind your own beeswax," I growled.

The dachsies were under the table looking for pickings. Both dogs stayed near Corky and me. Our eating habits were sloppier than the grownups and so business was better at our end of the table.

After dinner we settled down to a heavy game of canasta. It was Saturday and Mom wasn't too strict about our bedtime.

Granny was tired, and a little before ten we all said "Goodnight."

"Should I put Schnitzel's bed near yours?" I volunteered. Might as well be gracious about it.

"Oh no." Granny was firm on that subject. "She's your dog and belongs with you."

But Schnitzel didn't agree. No sooner was the house quiet, than she got out of bed and scratched at my door.

"Back to bed with you!" I ordered. "Didn't you hear what Granny said?"

But Schnitzel didn't listen and howled.

"Be quiet, you banshee. You'll wake everybody." I was getting mad.

Nothing helped.

I opened my door. She was out like a flash, and without a second's hesitation galloped to Granny's room. First she whined, then barked, and finally screamed to get in. But Granny didn't hear too well without her hearing aid and the door remained shut.

Schnitzel lay with her eyes glued to the crack and whined softly. She wouldn't even look at me.

"It's no good," I told her. "Come back to bed." It was impossible to stay angry.

Then she tried another tack. She ran downstairs and whined to be let out. I opened the front door and waited in the parlor. The house was cold, but the embers in the fireplace were still warm and I huddled in front of them. It seemed like hours, but Schnitzel did not return. I called to her, but there was no sign of the little dog.

I grabbed a coat from the hall closet, put some galoshes over my slippers, found a flashlight and tiptoed out of the house. It was freezing cold and eerily quiet. I shone the flashlight through the bushes, but nothing stirred. I called her again and again, but only my echo answered in the clear, cold moonlight.

Granny's car was standing in the shadows. It looked like a ghost. I peered in the window. The door was ajar. It creaked with frost. There, huddled next to the steering wheel lay Schnitzel, shivering, whimpering, but triumphant. She had figured that this was the only way to go home with Granny.

I picked her up gently and walked back to the house. She was cold, and in a way glad to see me. I held her close and couldn't help but feel sad. I carried her upstairs, quietly opened Granny's door, and let her slip in. She was Granny's dog and I had no right to her. I walked back to my room alone. It wouldn't be the same without her.

I threw myself on my bed, buried my head in my pillow and sobbed. If I had had any sense, I wouldn't have taken her in the first place. I'd let her have the run of my room, come to love her, and this is how it was to end. I never wanted another dog as long as I lived.

Chapter 10

Granny went back to town, but Schnitzel stayed. There was no other place for her to go.

She had come back to my room as if nothing had happened, looked for her bed, and planned to settle down. But I'd have none of it. I pushed her bed into the back hall and Corky more or less took charge of her.

Mom knew how I felt and said little, but Dad had a talk with me. One evening, instead of giving me his usual quick good night kiss, he plunked himself into the arm chair next to my bed. "Schnitzel's hurt your feelings," he started in, "and now you're all through with her. That's baby stuff. Grown-up people forgive and forget. Give her another chance. Someday you'll be glad that you did." He smiled at me with his wonderful crooked grin.

But I shook my head. "She walked out on me once and I don't want it to happen again."

"Suit yourself Bets." He kissed me good night and I could hear his footsteps disappearing down the hall. My room felt very empty.

I turned over and tried to sleep. I hoped it would snow during the night. Without Schnitzel I had time on my hands, and winter sports would keep me busy.

Part of my wish came true. It snowed—lightly, but not enough for skiing.

"Let's go for a walk, Bets," Corky suggested as we dumped our school books on the kitchen table the next afternoon. We've got an hour of daylight, and the woods look pretty with the snow."

I said okay. I had nothing better to do.

NO LOVE FOR SCHNITZEL

Corky whistled to the dogs, we tied woolly scarves around our heads, buttoned our jackets, and ran out into the sugary white pasture. It was brisk and beautiful. I was glad Corky had talked me into coming. It was good to be out.

The four setters ran ahead of us and then the dachshunds. We were heading for the woods and they were anxious to get there. Schnitzel followed Bitzel. She glanced back at me, but I pretended not to notice. Finally she gave up trying to be sociable and concentrated on keeping up with the big dogs.

The dachsies yipped after squirrels and occasionally a branch crackled as a setter burst through the underbrush. Our boots crunched over the powdery snow. Except for that, the woods were silent.

Last night's snow covered the ground and rested lightly on the evergreens as we crossed the small foot-bridge and headed toward the abandoned gravel pit. Nothing had really changed, but suddenly for no reason, I was afraid. "Let's go home,

Corks," I said in a small voice. "I'm getting cold."

Corky glanced at me and laughed. "Cold my foot! You don't like being so far away from the house. No one is going to bite you." And she started to sing the old Walt Disney tune, "Who's afraid of the big, bad wolf . . ."

I shivered. Something was very wrong.

The setters turned left toward the pit and hesitated. What had they heard?

Shaun, the bravest of the red dogs, advanced, and Eamon followed.

"Corks, Shaun's hackles are up!"

A low growl came from the gravel pit, then another and another.

Corky, white with terror, cried, "It's the wild dogs! Run Bets, run!"

But I couldn't. My knees had turned to jelly.

The Irish setters' hair stood straight up on their backs.

Long ago Mom had said, "If the Irishmen are along the wild dogs will never bother you." For a second it lessened my fear.

"Schnitzel! Bitzel!" I managed to call. Hearing the urgency in my voice they came running back.

That was all the wild dogs needed. They stormed out of the pit. There were dozens of them: police dogs, dobermans and great snarling mongrels. The setters took one look, tucked their tails between their legs and fled. Only the dachshunds remained. Corky grabbed Bitzel and headed for the nearest tree, but Schnitzel was out of reach.

"The tree! The tree!" Corky yelled, pointing to a gnarled oak.

I followed her blindly and somehow made it, scrambling up the rough trunk and tearing my legs as I climbed.

The pack closed in on Schnitzel. Corky, her one arm around Bitzel, managed to swing herself into an adjoining pine and hung precariously, six feet off the ground.

Only Schnitzel stood firm, growling her defiance. She knew that she was all that stood between us and the wild dogs.

The leader of the pack, a powerful police

dog, closed in, but Schnitzel did not retreat. She glanced back at me once as if to say, "I'll protect you," and then looked straight ahead. The rest of the pack stood by barking fiendishly. Their leader must have told them, "Lay off, this is my tidbit."

With one jump, the huge dog was on top of Schnitzel. He aimed for her throat, but missed and sank his teeth into her back.

Schnitzel yelled once in agony and terror, and then was silent.

Suddenly something snapped inside of me. I slid down the tree and grabbed the nearest good sized branch. Yelling at the top of my voice, I charged at the police dog. I beat him with all my might taking him completely off guard. He grabbed Schnitzel by the scruff of the neck and pulled her toward his lair. "Oh no you don't!" I screamed and hit him again. He dropped Schnitzel and ran, taking the pack with him.

I didn't want to look. Schnitzel was dead, and she had died protecting me.

I stood in a daze . . .

"Bets, snap to, we've got to get out of here. The pack may come back at any time."

"Schnitzel's dead," I answered tonelessly.

Corky, her coat and pants ripped and her hands bloody, stood next to me. Bitzel cowered near us. Directly in front of us lay Schnitzel.

I forced myself to walk over. She still breathed, but her back was torn open, her neck gashed and her front legs dangled at a crazy angle. I bent over her and she whimpered softly. The snow all around her was red with blood.

It was horrible.

"Bets, we've got to save her!" There was grim determination in Corky's voice.

I tore off my turtle neck, knelt down beside Schnitzel, and wrapped it around her bloody body. It didn't help much but it covered the gaping wounds and slowed down the bleeding.

"How'll we carry her? The less she's moved the better." It was all so hopeless that I began to cry.

"We'll make a stretcher." Corky was on the

ball now. She took off her windbreaker, zipped it, and laid it on the ground. Then, finding two straight branches, she stuck them through the side and sleeves of the coat.

"It'll work!" I was amazed.

We slid Schnitzel onto the stretcher and gently lifted her off the ground. She cried once and then was quiet. Much too quiet. I glanced at the blood-soaked sweater and shivered. Would she make it?

"You've got to hang onto the material and the poles, otherwise the whole works will unwind," Corky warned me.

I nodded and gritted my teeth, took a firm hold and kept in step with Corky. She was coatless and I was shirtless, but our thoughts were centered on getting Schnitzel home.

The winter wonderland had become a horror. The beautiful white snow was wet and slippery. The trees looked bleak and sinister, and behind every rock we imagined a wild dog shelter.

Schnitzel was a dead weight. Our arms ached and our feet slid, but we didn't dare put our burden down. The stretcher might collapse and then we'd be sunk. We pushed on with Corky in the lead and had stumbled back as far as the bridge when we saw Mom running toward us. "I knew something was wrong when the setters came back without you," she gasped.

"The wild dogs," I blurted out.

"Good Lord!" She dashed over to us.

"We're alright, but . . ." Corky pointed to Schnitzel.

Mom took one look and put her jacket over the injured dog.

"I'll rush ahead and bring the station wagon down the back road. Meet you at the top of the field. We'll have Schnitzel at the vets within half an hour." Mom was off, running up the path toward home.

She had given us hope, and although the rest of the way was uphill we made it quickly.

Mom met us as we struggled up the last incline. She opened the back of the station wagon and we lifted the stretcher into the car. I climbed wearily in beside Schnitzel and looked down at her closed eyes. I put my hand gently on her forehead and kissed her.

What a louse I'd been. I hadn't tried to understand her. I'd let her down when she needed me the most and this is how she repaid me. I couldn't look at her. I was too ashamed. Would I ever have the chance to make it up to her?

Chapter 11

Mom was in charge now . . . thank goodness for that! I felt limp and useless, but tried to hold the stretcher in one position as the car sped along the road. My eyes were closed and I could still see the wild dogs charging out of their lair. I forced my eyes open, stared straight ahead, and tried not to think.

Corky huddled in one corner of the front seat, her arms around Bitsy, pretending to doze. No one spoke. Only Schnitzel's labored breathing broke the uncomfortable silence.

It seemed forever until we finally pulled into the vet's yard. His helper was there to meet us. He picked Schnitzel up, stretcher and all, and carried her into surgery. Mom followed Schnitzel. Corky and I slumped down in the waiting room.

I heard her talking with Dr. Edwards, but I couldn't make out what was said. She came out shortly, looking grim. She was still jacketless. Her short hair was as dishevelled as ours, but her chin was as determined as ever.

"When Mom get's that look, beware," Dad often kidded. But today it made me feel better. Somehow she'd see to it that Schnitzel would be alright. She caught my eye and winked encouragingly. Suddenly the waiting room was more cheerful, and the smell of disinfectant not as stifling.

"We must look a fright. How about cleaning up a little, Corky?" I was beginning to unwind.

Corky nodded, "For once, you look worse than I do."

We washed our face and hands, combed our hair, and felt better for it.

We picked some magazines off the table and

tried to read "Dog World" and "Popular Dogs." A half hour went by, then another, and another.

"What's keeping him so long Mom?" I left the magazines on the sofa and wandered aimlessly about the room, fingering everything.

"Schnitzel is badly hurt. It'll take time to patch her up," Mom interrupted my wanderings. "You've got to have patience."

I looked at my watch, paced the floor, and wondered what was going on behind the closed doors.

And then my mood changed. I didn't want Dr. Edwards to come out. I didn't want him to tell us what I was sure would be bad news. I sat down and once again concentrated on not thinking. I was dead tired.

Finally the veterinarian emerged. He was tall, dark-haired, and serious looking. He spoke slowly with deliberation, "I've done all I can for your little bitch, Mrs. Benedict. She's still in shock, both her front legs are broken, and she's been badly mauled. But with a little luck, she may pull through."

"She's an old girl, you know," Mom told him worriedly.

"That's one of our problems." He stroked his small moustache thoughtfully. "We've given her a transfusion, set her legs, and sewn her up . . . ninety-eight stitches in all."

"Wow!" exclaimed Corky.

"The next few days will be critical. We'll give her massive doses of antibiotics and feed her intravenously. If she responds, she'll be out of danger in a week."

"May she come home then?" I interrupted.

"I'm afraid not. You'd better figure that she'll be here a month or more."

"May I come and see her?" I couldn't send a dog flowers or get well cards, and I wanted her to know that she hadn't been forgotten.

"I'm afraid not. We have found that visitors do more harm than good."

"Then may I say goodbye to her?" I started to cry again.

He shook his head. "She wouldn't know you. She's like a person who's just had an operation."

"But what happens if I never see her again?" I sobbed.

"You will, dear, you will." Mom put her arms around me and led me out to the car.

*   *   *

The first two weeks were the roughest. There were days when Mom didn't want to tell me what Dr. Edwards said. When I pressed real hard, the only thing I could get out of her was, "She's doing as well as can be expected."

We called daily at first, but after ten days the crisis passed and we knew she'd recover. From then on, every Thursday became "call Schnitzel day."

Six long weeks went by until the vet finally told us, "She's as well as I can make her. Her complete recovery is up to you. Pick her up tomorrow."

I was so excited that I spent the whole evening getting my room ready. I put her freshly washed bed next to mine, filled her private drinking bowl and arranged Granny's old scarf like a comforter. Then I broke out Granny's get well present. It was a box of dog candy and it looked like fudge. I put two pieces where I knew she would find them, next to her drinking bowl. She'll be real pleased with that, I decided. I felt good all over. I ran to the kitchen and checked up on her favorite dog food. Then I laid her collar and leash in the front hall and said good night to Mom and Dad.

"I have good news for you," Dad put down the newspaper. "The game warden caught up with the wild dogs and did away with them."

"They won't bother us again," Mom added.

"That's swell!" I breathed a great sigh of relief. I hadn't been in the woods since, and game warden or no, I had no intention of going back.

I sat down next to Dad. "Did you ever find out how the dogs got there?"

"No one can say for sure, but a good guess is that people abandon their pets. Some dogs get picked up, some die and some go wild. Of the wild ones, the fittest survive and join up with other homeless dogs. They live off garbage, deer, rabbits and crippled birds. They roam this whole area and it was just your bad luck to meet up with them." Dad lit his pipe. "Now don't worry about it anymore. The woods are safe again." But whatever

Dad said, Schnitzel and I would stay near the house.

"I'll pick you up after school tomorrow and then we'll bring Schnitzel home." I hugged Mom and Dad and happily wandered off to bed.

On Fridays school ended at one. However hard I tried, I couldn't concentrate and thought only of Schnitzel. Finally the dismissal bell rang. I ran for my coat and dashed out to the car.

Dr. Edwards' helper saw us as we entered. He smiled broadly, "I'll get your dog for you," he said. He took the collar and leash out of my hand and disappeared through the swinging doors.

I held my breath, shut my eyes tightly, and grabbed Mom's hand.

"Tell me when she's here," I whispered.

I heard footsteps and felt Mom touch my arm. I opened my eyes, ready to welcome Schnitzel, but all I saw was a beaten up, white haired old dog.

"That isn't Schnitzel!" I stammered.

The attendant nodded. "That's your dog, Miss."

Mom, too, looked taken aback.

I hesitated a second and then ran over to her. Her muzzle and paws were completely white and her back was an ugly mass of scars.

"Schnitzel, its me," I called.

She looked up slowly, hobbled painfully toward me, and tried to wag her tail. But the best she could do was lick my hand.

I picked her up, held her in my arms, and carried her out to the car. "Don't worry Schnitzel, old girl," I whispered. "We'll get you well in no time." But would we? I was far from sure.

Chapter 12

I knew it would take a long time, but I hadn't expected Schnitzel to come home a changed dog: lame, old and thoroughly dispirited. She wouldn't try to help herself and anything she was afraid of, she didn't attempt.

She was terrified of the stairs, and from the first day, she refused to go up and down them. Instead, she cried until someone came and carried her.

I spent hours persuading her. "Be sure she exercises her legs," the vet had told us. "It'll strengthen them." But she wouldn't.

I'd call and call to make her come to me, but all she would do was wag her tail, put her white head on her paws, and look at me with those pitiful eyes.

Whenever Corky walked down the stairs with Bitzel, in the hopes that Schnitzel would follow, Bitzel would double cross us and run back to sit with Schnitzel. She didn't understand what we were after and was no help at all.

If Bitsy would only play with her, but my sister's dog had gotten fat, lazy, and set in her ways. "What do you expect, she's not a puppy anymore?" Corky, as always, took Bitzel's part.

"Perhaps Schnitzel needs a playmate?" I was thinking out loud.

Corky snorted, "That's an idea, but not very practical. You'd better find something easier to cheer her up with."

Weeks passed. The scars became less raw and jagged. Her legs improved so that she walked with little or no limp, but her spirit remained broken and her nights filled with terror. Most dogs dream occasionally. They yip, twitch with excitement, and sometimes cry in their sleep. But since the attack, there'd hardly been a night that Schnitzel didn't howl. She'd wake me and I'd lean down and pet her. "It's all right, Schnitzel," I'd tell her. "There aren't any wild dogs here. You're in my room and no one is going to hurt you." But she'd shiver and shake until I lifted her into my bed. Then she'd snuggle up close, sigh once or twice, and go to sleep quietly.

A dog in my bed! Even Mom wouldn't believe that. It was a deep dark secret between Schnitzel and me. I made sure of that by carefully lifting her back into her basket when my alarm went off.

"You can't spend your life sleeping, Schnitzel," I told her one morning when she was still wrapped in Granny's shawl at noon. But she looked at me with her sad eyes as if to say, "What'll I get up for? Life's over for me."

I bought balls and rubber toys. I bribed her

with Granny's dog candy, but nothing interested her. If she hadn't let herself be attacked to protect me against the wild dogs, she'd still be her old self. Now it was up to me to repay her. Perhaps a pup would help. But where was I going to find one? A pup was my last hope.

On Saturday I took my Christmas money—twenty five dollars which I had been saving toward a bicycle—and walked over to Mrs. Dawson's on Bayberry Road. By car it didn't take long, but walking it was over an hour before the Dawson's kennel came into view.

I reached their gate posts, but was afraid to go in. I didn't know Mrs. Dawson well, and what would she say when I told her I wanted to buy a dog? She'd probably laugh and tell me that I didn't have enough money. Should I go back? I sure wanted to, but I turned into the drive-way, squared my shoulders, and strode past the big stone house toward the kennel.

The dogs heard me and started to bark. Dachshunds, poodles, corgis, and shelties jumped up and down in their wire runs, yipping their welcome.

I scraped up my courage and knocked at the kennel door.

"Come in," called a friendly voice. "I'm in the work room."

I found Mrs. Dawson trimming a cute gray poodle. She looked up and smiled her welcome and went on with her work. When she was finished, she stood him up and proudly said, "Here's my newest champion."

I nodded politely.

Mrs. Dawson wiped her hands on her blue jeans and looked at me more carefully. "You're Betsy Benedict, aren't you?"

"Yes Ma'am."

"What can I do for you?" Mrs. Dawson lived in a house with lots of servants, but she took care of the animals herself. "Did you come over to see my dogs?" Mrs. Dawson sounded pleased.

"Yes, sort of."

She picked up the poodle and put him back in

his kennel. "Any special ones you'd like to see?" She asked.

I nodded, "Dachshunds." I looked her straight in the eye and said, "I came to buy one."

"You came to do what?" I had taken Mrs. Dawson by surprise.

"I came to buy a dachshund puppy and I have money." I showed her the bills in my pocket. Then I told her Schnitzel's story and how I hoped a puppy would give my dog a new lease on life.

Mrs. Dawson was wonderful. She sat and listened, but I could see that she was thinking hard.

"I heard about Schnitzel and the wild dogs, but I didn't know about the problems you are having now. I'd like to help." She ran her fingers through her hair, lit a cigarette, and paced up and down.

"I have lots of money," I interrupted. "I have a whole twenty-five dollars."

"Let's not worry about the money. Let's find the right dog for Schnitzel."

NO LOVE FOR SCHNITZEL

I followed Mrs. Dawson outside. The weather was raw, but I felt warm and comfortable. At last I was doing something . . . something for Schnitzel.

There were dozens of dachshunds. Mrs. Dawson knew them all by name and as soon as we entered the run, they jumped all over her. She played with them and fondled their ears, but she seemed to be looking for a particular one.

I sat on the ground and let them swarm over me. Me, swamped by dogs and liking it. Who would have thought it? A peppy black one hopped into my lap and refused to budge. When another one tried to join her, she growled. She had adopted me.

"How do you like Fritzl?" Mrs. Dawson asked, pointing to my new-found friend. "She's three months old and full of the Old Nick."

"She sure likes me." I tried to push her away. She was chewing my hair, but all I succeeded in doing was to have her give my neck a good wash.

Fritzl was coal black and adorable. Her legs were short and stumpy. Her ears were long and the expression on her face was downright wicked.

"If you take me, I'll keep you hopping," she seemed to say.

I scrambled up. Fritzl or no, the ground was cold and it was time to shake the dachshunds out of my hair.

"Do you think Schnitzel would like her?" Mrs. Dawson pointed to my black shadow.

"She might be too wild for her, but she would certainly pep her up." I looked down. "Fritzl, leave my shoes alone," I commanded. "I'll need them for walking home!"

"Then you can have her. I had planned to make a show dog of her, but I have others, and helping a brave dog like Schnitzel is more important than a few dog show ribbons."

"But if she's a show dog, she's probably too expensive?"

Mrs. Dawson thought a minute. "I'm not going to sell her to you," she said very formally. "I'm giving her to Schnitzel. Spend your money on buying a bed, bowl, brush, and all the things that a fancy dachshund like Fritzl needs."

"Do you really mean it?"

Mrs. Dawson smiled. "I do. I am going to drive the two of you home. The walk may be okay for you, but it's too far for a young lady with such short legs."

She loaned me a collar and leash and we piled into her station wagon.

"Your Mother knows that you're over here."

"No," I said in a small voice, "but she loves dogs and she's been just as worried about Schnitzel as I have."

"Well, we're bringing her quite a surprise." Mrs. Dawson shook her head as she turned into our driveway. "If your Mother doesn't want Fritzl, I'll be glad to take her back."

Mom was at the door as we drove in. "Where have you been, Bets? I was beginning to worry." And then she saw Mrs. Dawson. "Thanks for bringing her home, Caroline. How did she get to your house?"

I could just feel what was going through Mom's

head. Dawson's . . . kennel . . . Corky perhaps, but Betsy wouldn't be caught dead with fifty or more dogs.

I opened the car door and Fritzl leaped out. A look of surprise and pleasure crossed Mom's face as she picked up the squirming sausage and hugged her.

"A play toy for Schnitzel," I explained. "She may cheer her up."

Mom looked suspiciously damp around the eyes. "I'm proud of you Bets," was all she said.

We dashed into the house and found Schnitzel lying in a patch of sunlight in the parlor. When she heard my footsteps, she wagged her tail feebly. Fritzl took one look, made a flying tackle, and landed on top of her.

Schnitzel tried to sit up. A horrified expression crossed her face. Should she run?

Fritzl woofed an invitation to play and wagged her tail invitingly.

Schnitzel, like a grandma putting up with her

granddaughter's capers, held her ground and let Fritzl swarm over her.

* * *

For the next few weeks, Fritzl took over the house, and nothing was safe. Anything that could be pulled or chewed was attacked: shoes, electric cords, legs of chairs, and rugs.

"Get that built-in rainstorm out of here," Dad would yell, and he was so right. Fritzl was definitely not housebroken and our rugs suffered. Thank goodness, downstairs, most of them were orientals. My room got the worst of it. In despair, we picked up the rug, sent it to the cleaner, and put it in storage.

But Schnitzel copied some of Fritzl's antics and gradually her spirit returned. When Fritzl took a shoe out of my closet, Schnitzel took the mate. The only difference was that Fritzl chewed on hers, while Schnitzel carefully buried hers under the covers. When Fritzl barked at an imaginary enemy, Schnitzel would too, and when Fritzl tore around the house, the old dog would follow as best she could. Gradually the nightmares became fewer and fewer.

"Bets, your room's a mess," Corky would tease me, but I chose to ignore her.

"That black monster is wrecking the house," Dad complained, but Mom was patient.

"She's no worse than the other dogs were at her age," she would pacify him, "and what she's doing for Betsy as well as Schnitzel is priceless."

I didn't quite know what Mom was talking about, but I knew that my brave Schnitzel was happy.

As Fritzl grew older, she became less of a tomboy, but she kept Schnitzel on the move. They roamed the gardens and the fields. They chased rabbits and dug for moles. Sometimes Bitzel joined them, but most of the time they remained a twosome.

Fritzl became everyone's favorite. Even Dad couldn't resist her bouncy ways and let her jump into his favorite chair. "You'll hurt Schnitzel's feelings if you make such a fuss over that brat," I'd warn him, but I really didn't mean it.

NO LOVE FOR SCHNITZEL

My room returned to normal. The rug never looked quite the same again, my book case was slightly chewed, and sometimes a shoe was missing, but I shared my room with Schnitzel and Fritzl, and they were wonderful.

Poor Corky had a dull time of it. Bitzel couldn't compete and became staid and stodgy.

"Do you think Mrs. Dawson might have a playmate for Bitzel?" Corky finally consulted me.

I felt very superior. "Don't know," I answered. "But let's walk over and pay her a visit."

ABOUT THE AUTHOR

Suzanne Wilding is a versatile young writer whose interests range from children's fiction to sporting and political subjects. Her first children's book, *Dream Pony for Robin*, was published by St Martin's Press in 1962. Grouse shooting in Scotland, the six top women in the UN Secretariat, and this country's first lady Under Secretary of State have all been subjects of past newspaper and magazine articles.

Miss Wilding received her B.A. from Barnard College. She lives with her husband, E. Albert Berol, and two daughters on a farm in Bedford Hills, New York.

6200 1